The Christmas Cobwebs

Retold by Lesley Sims

Illustrated by Ben Mantle

Reading consultant: Alison Kelly
Roehampton University

This story is about

Otto,

Otto's mother
and father,

Father Christmas

and seven spiders.

It was Christmas Eve.

"Hurry up, Otto!"
said his dad.

We're buying
the tree!

They set off for the
market.

The house was quiet.

Seven spiders came out
to play.

An hour later... Click!
The front door opened.

The spiders scuttled off
to hide.

Otto and his dad brought a huge tree indoors.

11

"Can we decorate the tree?" asked Otto.

"Look at the cobwebs!"
said his mother.

"First, we need to clean
this house."

Otto's dad swept.

Dust flew into the air.

Otto dusted.

Nasty spiders.
Shoo!

The spiders
ran up to the attic.

At last, the house was
ready for Christmas.

Late that night, the spiders crept downstairs.

The tree looked
magical.

"It's the perfect place
for us!" said the spiders.

18

They scurried
up the trunk...

...and ran along
the branches.

Just then, the room
started to shake.

Father Christmas shot
out of the chimney.

He saw the tree,
covered in cobwebs.

Oh no!

"Otto's mother won't like that," he said.

"But I can't upset the spiders."

He waved his hands...

The cobwebs became
glittering silver strands.

They looked beautiful.
People have put tinsel
on their trees ever since.

PUZZLES

Puzzle 1

Can you spot the differences between the two pictures?

There are six to find.

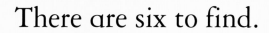

Puzzle 2
Can you put the pictures in order?

A

B

C

D

E

F

Puzzle 3

Choose the right speech bubble for the picture.

Answers to puzzles

Puzzle 1

Puzzle 2 - B F C E A D

B

F

C

E

A

D

Puzzle 3

About the story

The Christmas Cobwebs is based on a German folk tale.

Designed by Caroline Spatz

First published in 2012 by Usborne Publishing Ltd., Usborne House,
83-85 Saffron Hill, London EC1N 8RT, England. www.usborne.com
Copyright © 2012 Usborne Publishing Ltd.